A Richard Jackson Book

"Are There Any Questions?"

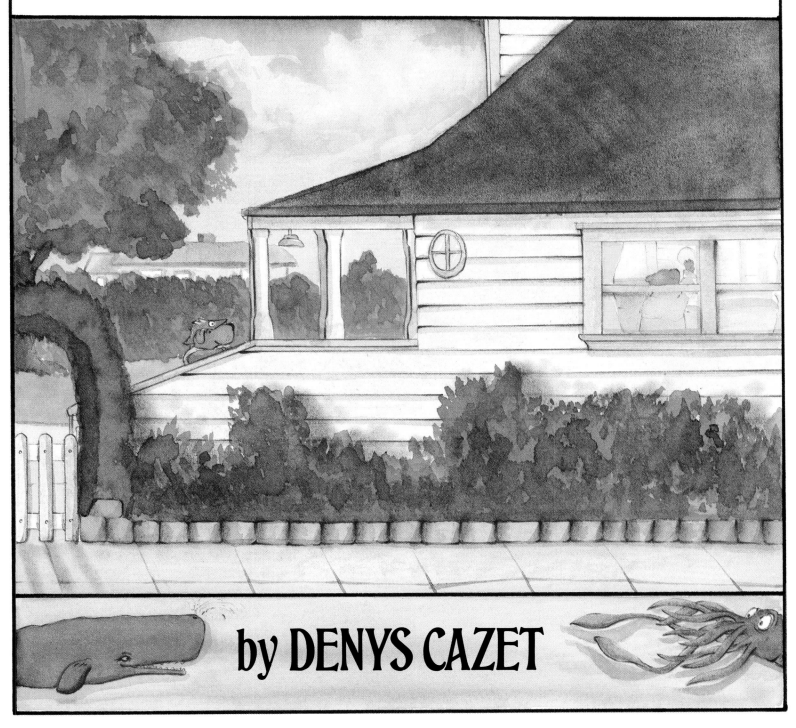

by DENYS CAZET

ORCHARD BOOKS • NEW YORK

Also by the author

Born in the Gravy
Dancing
A Fish in His Pocket
"I'm Not Sleepy"
"Never Spit on Your Shoes"
Night Lights: 24 Poems To Sleep On
Nothing at All

Orchard Books
95 Madison Avenue, New York, NY 10016

Manufactured in the United States of America. Printed by Barton Press, Inc.
Bound by Horowitz/Rae. Book design by Mina Greenstein.
The text of this book is set in 16 point ITC Bookman Light.
The illustrations are watercolor paintings, reproduced in halftone.

Hardcover   10 9 8 7 6 5 4 3 2
Paperback   10 9 8 7 6 5 4 3 2 1

Library of Congress Cataloging-in-Publication Data
Cazet, Denys.
Are there any questions? / by Denys Cazet.   p.   cm.
"A Richard Jackson book"—Half t.p. Summary: As Mother listens, Arnie,
a first grader, describes his class trip to the aquarium.
ISBN 0-531-30121-4 (tr.)   ISBN 0-531-07109-X (pbk.)
[1. Aquariums, Public—Fiction.   2. Mothers and sons—Fiction.]
I. Title. PZ7.C2985Ar 1992 [E]—dc20   91-42977

For my grandson,
TY

Arnie closed the screen door softly and tiptoed into the kitchen. He slipped up behind his mother and threw his arms around her.

"*Oh!*" she shouted.

"*Squid!*" shouted Arnie. "The deadly squid can squeeze a whale juiceless!"

"I'm not *that* big," said Mother.

She opened the refrigerator. "Tomato juice?"

"Milk, please," said Arnie.

"I love your new hat," said Mother. "Did you get it on the field trip?"

"The aquarium," said Arnie. "First grade only!"

Mother nodded and poured a glass of milk. "Well?" she said. "Tell me all about it!"

. . . name on your lunch and go to the bathroom.

"You have to put your name on your lunch," said Arnie, "go to the bathroom, and hand in your permission slip."

"That's a lot to remember," said Mother.

Arnie shrugged. "Some kids forgot."

But, I don't have to go.

I do, Helen.

Thanks, Arnie.

"I learned a new song on the bus," Arnie said. "I learned to count backward from one hundred!"

"My goodness," said Mother as she scooped up a handful of crackers.

"The balloon fish can eat a hundred times its own weight!" said Arnie. "Every day!"

Mother put the crackers back.

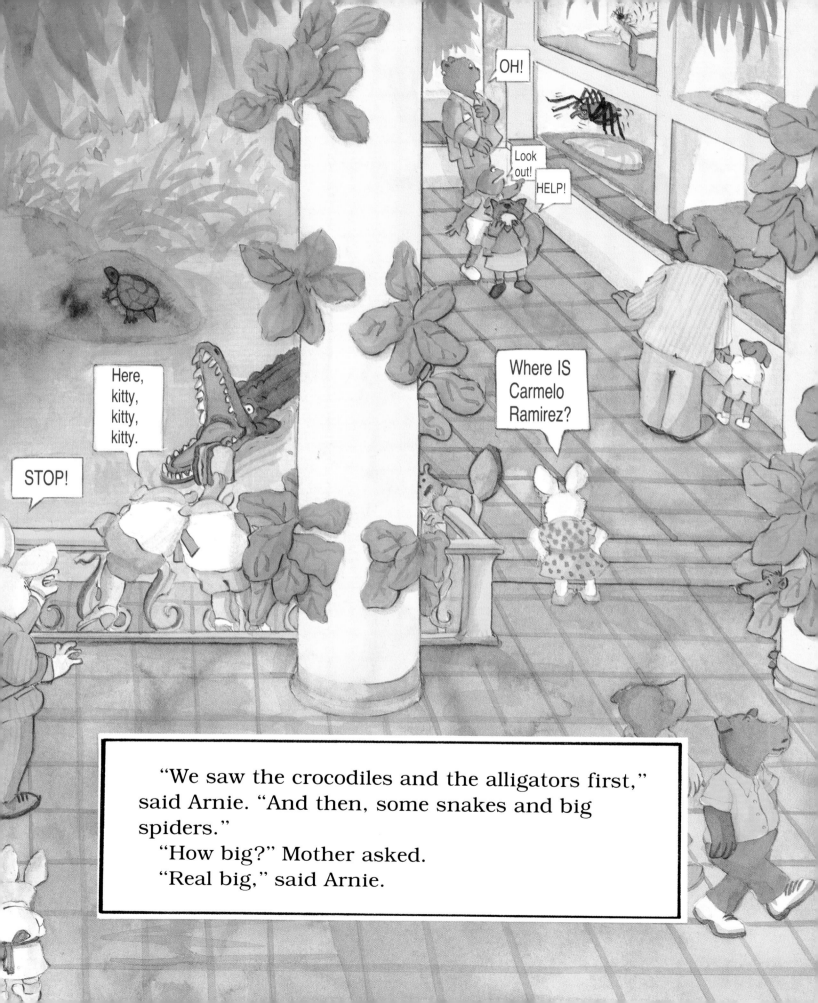

"We saw the crocodiles and the alligators first," said Arnie. "And then, some snakes and big spiders."

"How big?" Mother asked.

"Real big," said Arnie.

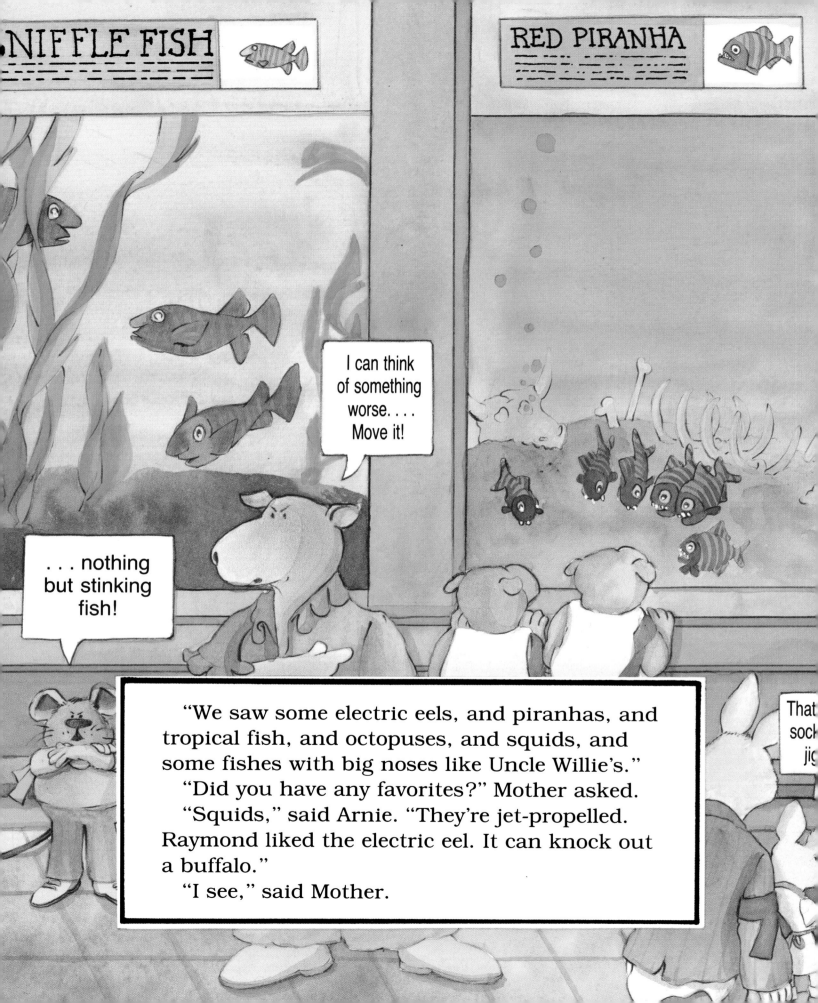

"We saw some electric eels, and piranhas, and tropical fish, and octopuses, and squids, and some fishes with big noses like Uncle Willie's."

"Did you have any favorites?" Mother asked.

"Squids," said Arnie. "They're jet-propelled. Raymond liked the electric eel. It can knock out a buffalo."

"I see," said Mother.

"We went into a room where the fishes went around and around and around and around and around," said Arnie. "My eyes got wobbly. I didn't feel so good."

Mother poured some more milk. "And now?"

"Okay," said Arnie. "Better than Raymond. He threw up."

"That's Raymond all over," said Mother. Arnie opened the refrigerator, and Mother took out some salmon croquettes. "Then what?"

Yum.

Brass is better.

"Then we went to the tide pool room," said Arnie. "The lady said we could touch anything we wanted."
"Did you?"
"Almost," Arnie said. "The starfish has suction cups on its feet. It can stick to your face."

Feeding time in the aquarium, boys and girls, a very special time . . .

"We watched them feed the dolphins," said Arnie. "I wanted to see them feed a giant squid. They have beaks and squeeze the living juice—"

"Out of you!" interrupted Mother. "Then what?"

"I guess they eat you," said Arnie.

Mother smiled. "What happened after the dolphins?"

"Oh," said Arnie. "Lunch."

No squids

Something's broken.

We can fix it. I'll show you.

Are you kids still on that dang bus?

Mother handed Arnie the dinner dishes. "Did you learn to count forward on the way home?" she asked.

"I can't remember," Arnie said. "It was very quiet."

Arnie's mother ran her fingers through his hair. "I'm glad you had a good day," she said.

"I did!" said Arnie. "I think the teacher did, too. She went home early."

Arnie picked up his hat. "I have to call Raymond," he said. "We have to plan our costume."

"Costume?" Mother said. "Why do you need a costume?"

"For the Halloween parade," Arnie said.

"Don't tell me," said Mother. "You and Raymond are going to be—"

Arnie threw his arms around his mother. "The deadly squid!" he said.

"Thank you," said Mother, "for not using the whale word."